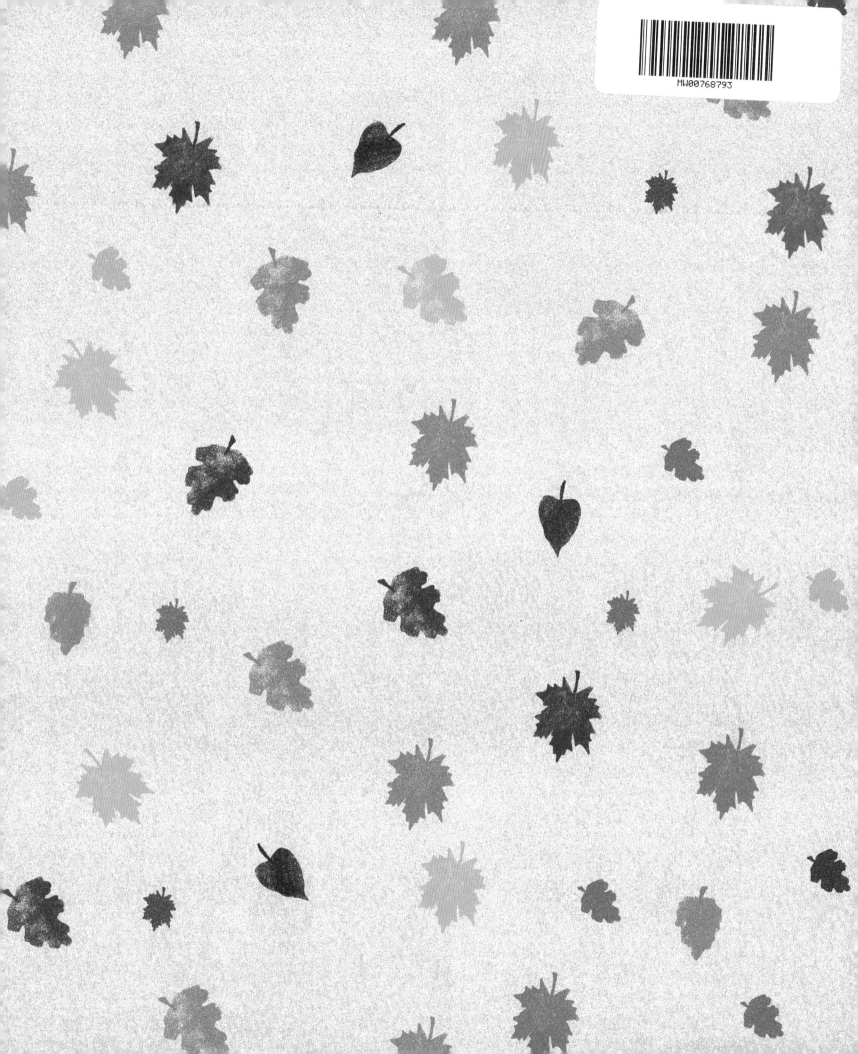

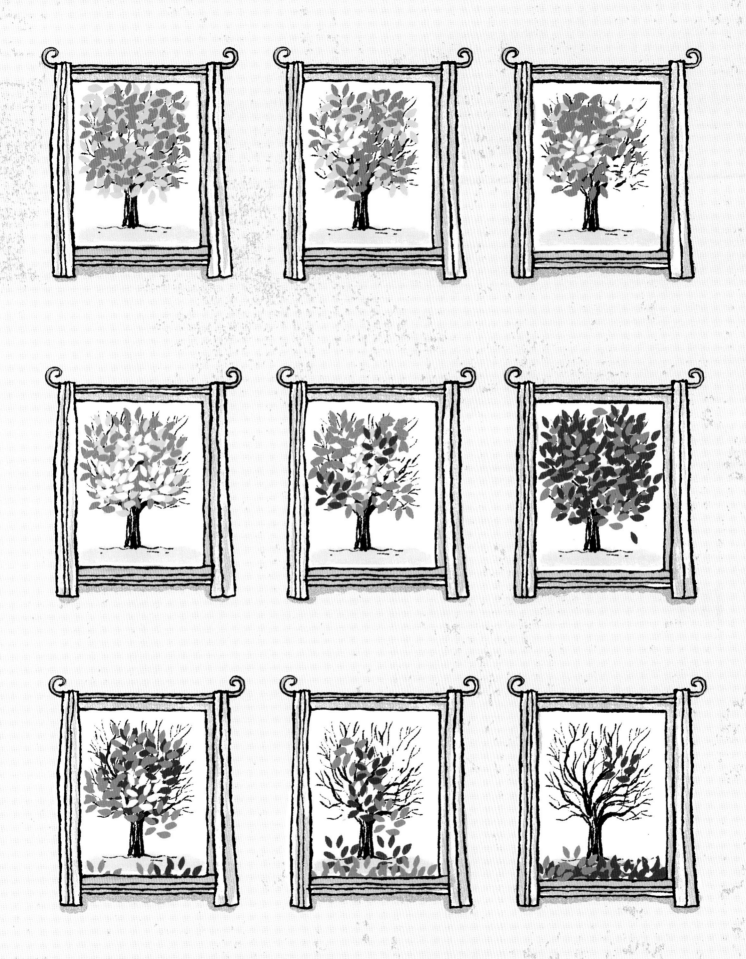

For Iz & Jo!

First Edition, June 2017
10 9 8 7 6 5 4 3 2 1
FAC-029191-17083
Printed in Malaysia

Designed by Maria Elias
This book is set in 18pt Trade Gothic LT Pro/Monotype
The illustrations were created with a #2 pencil and painted in Photoshop

Library of Congress Cataloging-in-Publication Data

Names: Neubecker, Robert, author, illustrator.
Title: Fall is for school / Robert Neubecker.
Description: First edition. | Los Angeles ; New York : Disney-Hyperion, 2017.
| Summary: "Two seasonally-opposed siblings face the end of summer with
both joy and dread. But as Sister shares her enthusiasm for fall, school,
and everything they encompass, Brother's own excitement grows in this
celebratory picturebook"—Provided by publisher.
Identifiers: LCCN 2016022965| ISBN 9781484732540 (hardcover) | ISBN
1484732545 (hardcover)
Subjects: | CYAC: Stories in rhyme. | Schools—Fiction. | First day of
School—Fiction. | Autumn—Fiction. | Brothers and sisters—Fiction.
Classification: LCC PZ8.3.N3676 Fal 2017 | DDC [E]—dc23
LC record available at https://lccn.loc.gov/2016022965

Reinforced binding

Visit www.DisneyBooks.com

Fall Is For School

ROBERT NEUBECKER

Disney • HYPERION

LOS ANGELES   NEW YORK

Fall is time for school!

That really is uncool.

Fall is here! It's time for school!
The summer's in the past.

I'm staying here. I will not go.
Vacation went too fast.

Fall is time for turning leaves;
the weather's growing cool.

**Fall is here! Come on with me!
It's time to go to school!**

School is really not my thing.
You go on alone.
I'll be fine all by myself,
sitting here at home.

Let's go and meet your teacher;
you're going to look so nice.
Tuck in your shirt and tie your shoes!

You must take my advice!

Teacher! Teacher? Sister, no!
I do not think that I can go!

In school we'll learn of Romans,
who really were no dummies,
and the pyramids in Egypt,
all filled up with mummies!

Dinosaurs and carnivores,
mighty tyrannosaurus,
giant tigers, woolly mammoths

really were enormous!

I am going to play all day!
It doesn't matter what you say!

Recess is for playing games:
We'll run and jump and climb!
Let's go right now and join the fun.
You really must not whine!

Whine.

Do your numbers! 1, 2, 3!
Add, subtract, and multiply.
**A million, trillion—my, oh my!
Count the stars up in the sky!**

I do not like arithmetic!
It hurts my eyes!
It makes me sick!
I will not go, I do not care.
I have heard enough.
To tell the truth,
I'm not like you.
School is just too tough.

Rocket ships that fly to Mars,
music, sports, and art.
These are all the things you love. . . .
I think you're very smart!

We will learn to read and write;
the stories we will tell!
And if you want to do it right,
you have to learn to spell!

Fall is time for parties,
for spooky Halloween.
We'll dress up just like zombies
and paint our faces green.

In science we will never stop
until we ace the pumpkin drop!

Pumpkin drop?

Pumpkin drop!
We pad them up and drop them.
It's really engineering.
If your pumpkin doesn't smash,
the teacher will be cheering!

Is that something I can do?
And everyone is going?
Staying home day after day
was getting kind of boring.

Fall is time for school!
We'll learn, and we'll be clever.
A great big world will open up
and change our lives forever.

Maybe school will be all right.
I might just reconsider.
Maybe you are not so dumb, for my baby sister.
Fall is time for school!